Christopher and the Bouncing Beagle, 1st Edition (Hardcover).

Story concept, text, and illustrations by © 2024 Leanne Staback, Ph.D.

Editing, print preparation, formatting, back cover summary, cover and interior design provided by Staback Author Services.

Books may be ordered through popular, online retailers, the publisher's online store, IngramSpark, or by contacting the publisher at:

Page Turner Books, Inc.®
170 S. Green Valley Pkwy., Suite 300
Henderson, NV 89012-3145

Visit our website at www.ptbooksinc.com or contact us via email at contact@ptbooksinc.com.

Page Turner Books, Inc.® name and logo/imprint are copyright of Page Turner Books, Inc.®

Hardcover ISBN: 978-1-958487-30-3
Paperback ISBN: 978-1-958487-34-1
Ebook ISBN: 978-1-958487-35-8

Printed in the United States of America. First printing: July 2024.

ATTENTION CORPORATIONS AND ORGANIZATIONS!
Most Page Turner Books, Inc.® publications are available at quantity discounts with bulk purchase for educational, business, or sales promotional use. For information, please visit www.ptbooksinc.com or http://ingramspark.com or call (702) 606-1775.

Christopher and the Bouncing Beagle

Leanne E. Staback, Ph.D.

PAGE
TURNER
BOOKS INC.

Henderson, NV, USA

Children's Books by Leanne E. Staback, Ph.D.
(Coming in 2024)

"Around the World with St. Nicholas and Friends"
Vol. 1 of 12 in the new "Around the World" Series

"The Brave Little Dreamer"

"Christopher and the Bouncing Beagle"

"Marc the Viking and the Wily Wolf"

"Sloane the Smiling Sloth"

"Shawn and the Lion's Roar"

"Steven the Sea Turtle's Big Adventure"

For my son Christopher,

Britainy the First

and

Britainy the Second.

In a cute little town,
With a cobblestone street,
Lived a boy named Christopher,
So kind and sweet.

With a twirl of his hat
And a smile so bright,
He'd stroll through the town
From day until night.

Christopher had a friend,
A beagle so true,
A sweet pup named Britainy,
Who had just turned two!

Through the town they'd go,
Greeting friends as they went..

One day at the park,
While enjoying the sun,

Christopher had a plan,
To teach Britainy some fun!

"I'll teach my pup
A trick so grand,
She'll bounce and leap
Across the land!

So off they went,
With a smile and a cheer,

To an open space
Where the grass was clear.

Christopher showed Britainy, how to leap across grass,

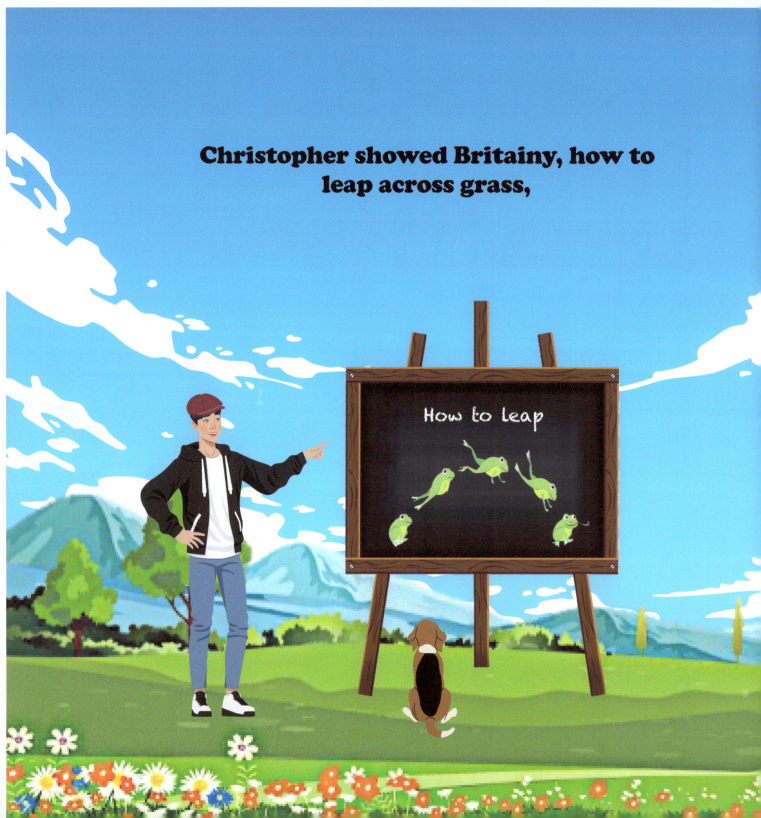

How to bounce and to jump,
Oh, what a blast!

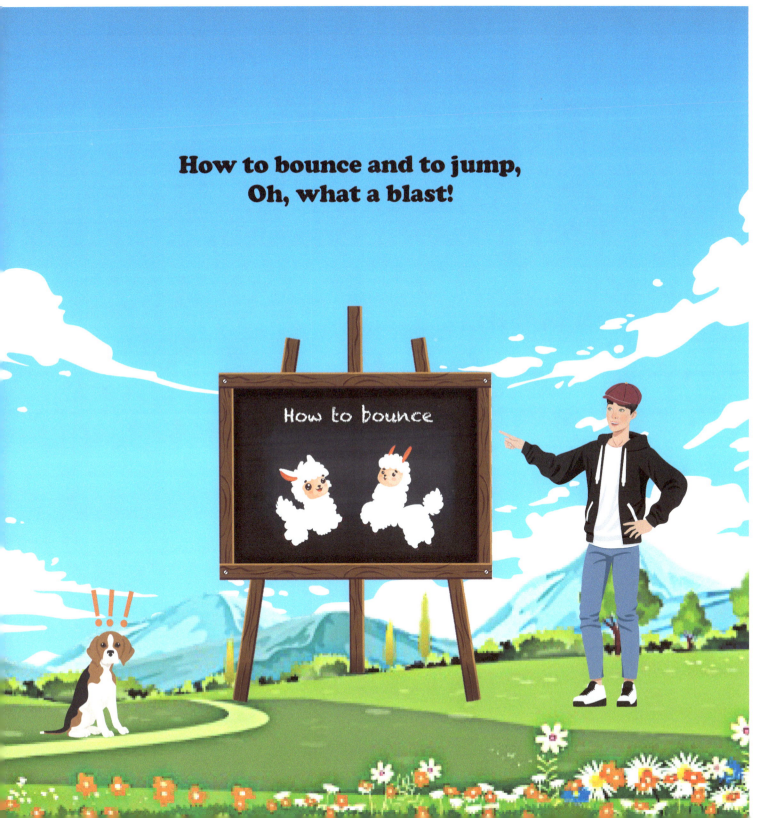

But Britainy,
with a tilt of her head,
Looked at Christopher,
with eyes of dread.

She wagged her tail
Nervous about the plan,
As if to say,
"I don't know if I can."

Christopher smiled
With a twinkle in his eye,
And said to his friend,
"Come on, Britainy, would I lie?"

He took a ball,
And gave it a soft toss,

Then with a bark and a leap, She
was off without pause.

Britainy was so excited
She ran right past the ball!

She looked stumped at Christopher
And gave a little howl.

Behind her, she heard the ball
Hit the ground again.
So, she turned round and chased it
To catch it for her friend.

She jumped and she leaped,
With a bounce so high,

As Christopher watched
With pride in his eye.

Through the park they played,
In a manner so sweet,

Inviting folks who watched,
Making friends with those they'd meet.

The townsfolk watched with a
laugh and a clap,
For in Christopher and Britainy,
Joy was a snap.

As the sun set low
In the sky so bright,
Christopher knew
It was time for goodnight.

He patted Britainy
With a gentle hand,
And said, "Well done,
My bouncing friend!"

Christopher remembered
Britainy's funny routines.
He smiled at her sleeping,
And wished her sweet dreams.

And sweet dreams to you too, my friend!